Does Anybody Love Me?

For Rachel G.L.
To Avril R.B.

Text copyright © 2002 Gillian Lobel
Illustrations copyright © 2002 Rosalind Beardshaw
This edition copyright © 2002 Lion Hudson

A Lion Children's Book
an imprint of
Lion Hudson plc
Mayfield House, 256 Banbury Road,
Oxford OX2 7DH, England
www.lionhudson.com
ISBN 0 7459 4571 6

First edition 2002
3 5 7 9 10 8 6 4

A catalogue record for this book is available
from the British Library

Typeset in 16/24 Baskerville BT
Printed and bound in Singapore

Does Anybody Love Me?

Gillian Lobel

Illustrated by
Rosalind Beardshaw

LION
Children's Books

Charlie was making chocolate
pudding. She put some dark
crumbly earth into the mixing bowl.
She added a handful of pebbles for currants and
a sprinkling of sand for sugar.

Then she went to the kitchen, turned on the cold tap
and watched her pudding go soft and squidgy.

She gave it a really good stir.

Chocolate pudding flew all round the kitchen.
'Oh, Charlie! What a mess!'
Dad looked really cross. 'That was a silly thing to do.'
'I'm making chocolate pudding for
Grandpa!' Charlie felt hurt.
'You're making a mess!' grumbled Dad.
Charlie stomped upstairs. She wouldn't
give Dad any of her pudding.

She decided to play boats in the bathroom. She filled the basin full of water and sailed the bath-time boats round their little lake.

'Now there's a big storm coming!' She stirred the water hard. Little waves splashed over the soap.

'Crash!' She smacked the water hard for thunder. The waves rolled over the basin and poured onto the carpet.

'Oh, Charlie!' Mum stuck her head round the door. 'You've soaked the carpet – and look at your socks! Not like my sensible girl at all.'

'Nobody in this house loves me!' cried Charlie. She ran into her bedroom and threw herself on the bed. 'I'll run away,' she said crossly. 'Then they'll be sorry.'

She took a little suitcase from under her bed. She put in a sweatshirt and a woolly hat. Then she picked up Panda and tucked him under her arm.

'We're going somewhere nice,' she told him, 'where there's no cross people.'

Charlie went into the kitchen. She took some cookies from the jar and a carton of juice from the fridge. She squashed them into her suitcase.

Then she went out of the front door.

She sat down on the front doorstep.
Where should she go?
'I know, I'll run away to the jungle. They'll never find me there.'

She went round to the back of the house. At the
bottom of the garden there was a dark tangle of laurel
bushes. You had to crawl through a little
tunnel to reach the secret hiding place.
The laurel leaves smelled sharp
and sweet. Silver cobwebs stuck to
her hair and pinged her
nose softly.

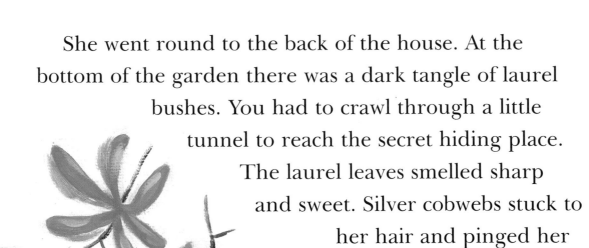

Then she was there, at her favourite place. You couldn't see the house at all. Tall fir trees made a secret den where their branches bent low to the ground, and in the corner there was a tumble of little rocks. She crept through the curtain of shivering fir.

'Now we'll have a party,' she told Panda.

They shared the cookies and the juice.

Then they played shipwrecks. Charlie was the captain, and Panda was the ship's monkey. Charlie splashed through the green waves, holding Panda safely out of the water, until she reached a desert island.

'We must find water,' she cried. They sat down and pretended to drink.

It was fun, but she was really thirsty now. There was no more juice in the carton, and Panda was beginning to whimper.

Suddenly a drop of water landed on her hand.

'It's raining!' shouted Charlie. 'We're saved, Panda!'
She stuck out her tongue to catch the drops. The rain
was warm and sweet, but not enough.

It went very dark under the fir trees. Charlie
shivered.

'Don't worry, Panda,' she said.
'I'll look after you.'

Rain trickled down the back
of her neck, and her skin went
cold and bumpy.

Suddenly there was a flash of lightning. Charlie
grabbed Panda and held him tight.

'I want to go home!' shouted Panda.
'We can't,' said Charlie.
'Nobody loves us any more.'
In the bushes
something crackled.
The noise got closer.
Twigs snapped, and
Charlie could hear
breathing!

Then a head stuck through the secret passage.
It was Grandpa's.

'Oh, Charlie,' he panted. 'I'm so glad I've
found you – I'm lost in the jungle, and I don't
know how to find my way home!'

'Don't worry,
Grandpa.' Charlie
hugged him
tightly. 'I'll save
you – just follow me!'

She and Panda took
Grandpa all the
way home.
'Oh, thank
goodness you've
found Grandpa!' said
Mum, giving her a hug. 'That's my brave girl!'
Then Charlie led Grandpa into the warm kitchen and
gave him a lovely big helping of chocolate
pudding.

More picture stories
from Lion Children's Books

My Very First Bedtime Book   *Lois Rock and Alex Ayliffe*

On the Day You Were Born   *Sophie Piper and Kristina Stephenson*

Who Made Me?   *Shirley Tulloch and Cathie Felstead*